The Mystery of Baxter Mansion

A Detective Thriller
by Steve Presley ©

All the characters, action, and the places used in this tale were fictitious.  No living human alive or passed away was characterized.  Although cities and places were mentioned, no attempt was made to accurately describe them.  The events, locales, and persons mentioned were created from the writer's imagination.  They were not real or actual.  This was a work of pure fiction.

Chapter List.

Chapter 1. Baxter Mansion

A single lane dirt road crossed miles into the country.  A paved driveway left the dirt road passed tall gray stone wall through a wooden gate, curved left then straightened for about a quarter of a mile.  A forest was all around.  A lake came up on the right.  It was a long oval shape.  A swift stream entered and left the lake to supply it with water.  The road curved right into a clearing where the mansion came into sight.  The drive turned into a large circle just in front of the front porch and door.  The driveway joined the traffic circle directly opposite from the mansion.  There was room to the outside of the circle to park several cars.  In the center of the circle was a five-tiered fountain.  Water sprouted six feet up into the air to fall and splash on the five basins below.  Several large wooden benches sat on the lawn on both sides.

Slue sky was up above the landscape.  Puffy white clouds were gliding along in the bright golden sunlight.  It was a slightly warm day.

A large wooden sign was to the right.  It had a gray field with black letters that read, "Baxter Mansion."  This was a large three-story gray granite building.  There was a Gothic influence to it.  Somehow the Georgian Classical Grecian style was present as well.  The sign also has a coat of arms.  These were the trappings that came from the fifteenth century when knights rode to war in armor on large horses.  It had a silver helmet at the top that had a long yellow plume.  Two crossed red spears with golden points were underneath.  The shield was white with five blue stars crossing diagonally downwards.  A red heart was on the upper right side.  A golden diamond was on the lower left side.  The mansion was an immense structure that was quite impressive to look upon.  There were five windows on each side of the glossy black front door.  This was a total of thirty windows on the front wall.  The roof was red clay tile.  There was a copula in the center with a copper domed crown.  It was reddish with green patina where oxidation happened from standing moisture.  There were six glass windows about it where a view of the landscape was to be taken in.  The window frames were painted white giving a fresh and clean appearance to the structure.  Eleven marble steps led up from ground level to the doorway.  Tall well-clipped boxwood hedges framed the perimeter of the foundation.  They were square cut.  Some colorful flowers bloomed in beds just outside of the hedges.  A flock of about thirty doves flew about the rooftop and trees in graceful arcs swooping about in a free and peaceful manner.  The building was tee shaped with a perpendicular portion extending back from the front.  On either side of this back portion were carefully manicured courtyards.  Several marble sculpture pieces stood to create a classical effect.  Each had s fountain similar to the one in front but smaller.  The woods surrounded the building but a large enough green grassy lawn existed to provide the necessary separation so that the mansion was not crowded but stood on an open field all its own.

The mansion was miles away from any other building located far out into the rustic countryside.  It being where it was seemed unlikely but there it was just the same.

If here was a placed named the Baxter Mansion, then there should be a Mr. Baxter. Yes, indeed, there was. He was Mr. Robert Baxter. He was called Robin for short. Mr. Robin Baxter. He was a senior gentleman aged 82. Mr. Baxter was average in size being 5 foot 7 inches tall and 160 pounds in weight. His red hair had all become gray and later white with age. He was bald at the back of his head. The red hair earned him the nickname Robin. He had brown eyes and bushy eyebrows above them. His face seemed both kind and serious. It was squared at the chin, cheeks, temple bones, and forehead. Robin had thick bones that made him look sturdy and strong. Speaking, he had a pleasant voice that used inflections that added feeling to what he said. He was calm and cheerful. He had a temper but seldom was it seen. Most of the time he wore clean dark suits with white shirts and conservative ties. Other times he wore knit shirts and black or brown cotton trousers. His lace-up shoes were usually brown, black, or oxblood. Hr preferred cotton or nylon socks. He seemed to be a most neat and energetic individual ready to speak to or help anyone. Quite retired was he living daily to leisure and very restful activities, as he worked no longer. He had earned all the necessary finances when he was a younger fellow. Mr. Baxter was a very rich elderly man. He had spent his career as a commodity broker. This was like a stock or a bond broker but dealt in different substances like feed, food, and raw minerals and materials. This caused him to travel widely all over the globe. As a result he visited China trading in rice. He went there on many trips. In his house he had a Chinese room with items he found in that large ancient Oriental land. Mr. Baxter collected chinaware, art, sculpture, fabrics, and furniture. Liking the quiet restful character he built this home well away from city life. It had a variety of rooms and features.

Game Room-This had a billiard table, bowling, card games, board games, roulette, shuffleboard, a wooden toy castle with metal knights and soldiers, darts, and a target range for pistols and rifles, powered by compressed air and not gunpowder.

Ballroom-This had a large dance floor with a grand piano and a band stage. Other party events or celebrations were at times held here. Sometimes musical expositions were held in concert in this room.

Chinese Room-This had Oriental wallpaper, glass and china, rugs, toy dolls, Oriental furniture, paintings, woven bamboo items, large elaborately painted vases with colorfully died paper flowers in them, Chinese robes and costumes to wear, and three suits of armor with weapons.

Lounge-This had large glass windows. There were four couches, eight stuffed armchairs, a refreshment counter, and a bar. Mr. Baxter did not drink alcohol as it hurt his stomach. He would mix them for others as a gracious host.

Kitchen-This had the necessary usual appliances, two food preparation tables, 7 chairs, three sinks in the counter, storage cabinets, food shelves, many pots, pans, china, and glassware pieces.

Living Room-This had five couches, ten arm chairs, six wall mirrors, five end tables, a desk and chair, a spinet piano, several lamps, sculpture pieces, and paintings hung from the walls.

Dining Room-There was a banquet sized table with twenty chairs, four china cabinets, three buffet tables holding silverware, wooden bowls, candles, and various dining accessories, two large mirrors, four crystal and brass chandeliers, and three side tables to hold food to be served.

Library Study-This had many books in bookshelves, study tables with chairs, three couches, six stuffed armchairs, numerous lamps, a large globe, wood paneled walls, and two side rooms containing a theater and an art gallery. This was Mr. Baxter's sometimes business office.

Conservatory-This was a glassed in room like a greenhouse with translucent stained glass. Much light came into this room. Numerous plants were growing in a variety of containers. There were tables, chairs, a gray tiled floor, cabinets that stored a wild variety of things, several birdcages with chirping colorful birds, and one large desk with a chair where paperwork, writing, or reading may be done. Past a set of double doors was an outdoor terrace, with a hot spa pool nearby, and farther out a tennis court.

Bathrooms-They each had sinks, toilets, bathtubs, medicine cabinets, a towel closet, and a thick rug on the floor.

Bedrooms-Fifteen bedrooms were in the mansion. They had beds, chest of drawers, a mirrored dresser, a desk and chair, bookcases, table and floor lamps, a small dining table with two chairs, comfortable arm chairs, lacy window curtains, Oriental rugs over thick pile carpet, tasteful wall paper, and framed paintings hung on the wall. Each room was different. Some had a sauna as well.

Main Hallway-This led to the living room. It had an Arabian rug on the floor and some small side tables with hand painted vases on them. Each vase has fresh flowers in it.

Garage-It was built to hold seven cars. There was an exercise room with weights to lift there. A workshop had tools needed for many tasks. The cars stood on carpeted over cement floors. There were two sedan cars, a bus, two sports cars, a black limousine, and an antique touring car.

Robin Baxter had lived a life of dollar signs aimed at wise purchases and clever trading to create a profit margin that gave him much wealth. He kept good business record books, met and dealt with people wisely, and earned a generous gain at about any venture that he undertook.

There were five servants who lived and worked there.  They were these people:
Mrs. Butterworth  the cook.  She played classical violin at dinner sometimes.
Mrs. Fastidiousness  the maid
Mr. Greenthumb  the gardner
Mr. Roadway  the chauffeur
Mr. Proper  the butler

These were only nicknames created to describe the type of work that they did.  Their real names were Agnes Adamson, Constance Collier, Henry Hudson, Edward Austin, and Chester Wainwright.

Mrs. Butterworth, (the cook) aged 50, was only 5 feet tall and weighed 110 pounds.  She had chestnut hair that she kept tied to the top of her head.  Her dark brown eyes matched her hair color well.  Being religious and having a good memory, frequently she quoted Bible verses.  Everything about her was neat and proper.  She handmade all of her clothing.  Her baked bread was heaven on earth.

Mrs. Fastidiousness (the maid) was age 39, was 5 feet 8 inches tall, and weighed 160 pounds.  She had curly blonde hair that came down to below her knees.  Her green eyes glistened in the daylight.  She had talent playing cards and was difficult to beat.  Her alto singing voice was very pleasant.  She knew many songs by heart, but she could not read any music.

Mr. Greenthumb (the gardener) was a very ugly person with a nice gentle personality that everyone liked.  When people first met him they were frightened, but getting to know him, this fear soon left.  He was aged 64, was 5 feet 7 inches tall, and weighed 160 pounds.  He could whistle well and was a tap dancer.  He was black headed and had brown hair.  He had a pet collie dog named Pete that stayed with him.

Mr. Roadway (the chauffeur) had red hair and green eyes.  He could juggle ten grapefruits expertly.  He was aged 49, was 6 feet tall, and weighed 185 pounds.  He had a gray tabby cat named Oscar.  This man had excellent vision and saw well at night.  Being superstitious, he kept a four-leaf clover in his pocket.  It was wrapped in wax paper and taped over several times with clear cellophane tape.  It must have brought him good luck because he never had a traffic accident.  From time to time, he smoked large strong smelly cigars.

Mr. Proper (the butler) was aged 50, had brown hair and blue eyes, was 5 feet 11 inches tall, and weighed 185 pounds.  He was a ventriloquist who could make his voice come out of about anything.  He played classical piano with an expert ability.  Something special was about him that made him most pleasant to be with.  This was due to his personality, charm, manner, and respectful way of speaking.  He loved to eat peanuts.

Liking the company of others, Robin Baxter entertained several stay-in guests.  They were distantly related people being fourth to sixth cousins who knew each other and got along very well.  He spent time with the talking, serving refreshments and food, and holding enjoyable events.

The six guests were the following people:
Israel Sterling  was a wealthy banker
Bunny Brompton  was a big real estate man
Florey Filshingham  was a fashion model and theater actress today a socialite
Bertram E. Hadley  was the owner of ocean shipping and mining, a billionaire
Elbert Chessman  was a retired Army general who owned chains of hotels and restaurants
Wyckham Forsythe  was a prosperous railroad and trucking magnate

Each had a separate second floor bedroom with an adjoining private bathroom.  They had a choice of eating in the dining room or having it served in their bedroom.  They might meet with the others for chitchat or entertainment.  A description of the guests follows.

Israel Sterling (a wealthy banker) looked in every way average.  His black hair was neatly combed.  He had a pale white complexion.  Israel's gray eyes were intelligent and honest looking.  His voice was a high baritone that seemed joyful and content.  Mr. Sterling was 5 feet 11 inches tall and weighed 180 pounds.  He was 48 years old.  Comfortable sport clothing he wore accented his active personality.  Mr. Sterling was a talented landscape painter.

Bunny Brompton (a big real estate man) was a husky brute of a man who was well coordinated for his size.  There was something of a lumberjack in him, as he seemed to be an outdoor type.  Thick brown hair covered his head.  His brown eyes gazed out at the world.  His real name was Robert.  This was Bob for short.  Somehow the nickname Bunny was given to him.  His hands and arms were large stemming from his big bony structure.  His passion was weight lifting.  At 62 years of age, he 6 feet 2 inches tall and weighed 230 pounds.

Florey Filshingham (a fashion model and theater actress today a socialite) was a blessed with natural endowments that made her quite a beautiful woman.  Being tall, slender, and graceful, blessed with a lovely face, teeth, and hair, she was attractive.  Intelligent, she used well-spoken word combinations to express herself.  Florey dressed well which supplemented her charm.  She was quite photographic and belonged on a stage as a model or actress.  The shape, contour, and coloring of her lips were lovely.  There was sophistication to her manner that told she was from the upper class.  Florey was a fashion model and theater actress today a socialite.  Lady Filshingham at age 45, weighed 130 pounds and was 5 feet 10 inches tall.  She had red hair and green eyes.  Playing the flute well, she also was an accomplished ballet dancer.

Bertram E.Hadley (the owner of ocean shipping and mining, a billionaire) looked like a clerk accountant being a person of small delicate frailty. He seemed to be suited to counting money and listing assets in columns. Mr. Hadley was baldheaded and had a rounded face. The hair he did have was at one time black but now was gray. Bertram was aged 67 years, was 5 feet 6 inches tall, and weighed 150 pounds. His stooped over shoulders were due to his being in his late sixties. He loved fine food and alcoholic refreshments. Chocolates and hard candy were something that frequently went from his hand into his mouth.

Elbert Chessman (a retired Army general who owned chains of hotels and restaurants) had a square jawed with a block shaped head. His face had coarse rugged features. Wide shoulders and tiny hips made him took top heavy. His deep bass voice was a booming experience to hear. He was blonde headed with brown eyes. Ebert aged 55 years, was 6 foot 4 inches tall, and weighed 240 pounds. He commonly smoked a pipe and was fond of fried seafood. He played tennis and golf like a professional.

Wyckham Forsythe (a prosperous railroad and trucking magnate) had dark olive skin, black hair, and light blue eyes. Being 5 feet 9 inches tall Mr. Forsythe weighed 170 pounds and was age 70. He liked to read mystery novels and smoked Turkish cigarettes. Wyckham was an avid fisherman and hunter. Likewise he liked to go hiking and camp out of doors when the weather was suitable. This man had amassed a large and valuable stamp and coin collection. Wyckham Forsythe had traveled the world many times.

Robin Baxter spent solitary time with contemplational prayer with no words, just relaxation. He also listened to classical music recordings. There were several nearby hiking trails and a rowboat for the lake to enjoy. There was decent fishing available there too.

Chapter 2.  Missing Possessions and Persons

The police building was in the center of the nearby town next to the courthouse and jail.
It was a two story stone building.  Double front doors led to a wide hallway.  Police
offices and meeting rooms were here.  A large locker room and shower was to one side at
the end.  Police Chief Wilson Wallace had an office at the front.  It had two windows, a
gray meal desk and chair, two bookcases, three stuffed armchairs six wooden chairs, a
flag on the wall, and various framed photographs of him and policeman here and there.
Chief Wallace was 5 feet 9 inches tall and weighed 230 pounds.  His close cropped
blonde hair was slowly becoming gray.  Two baby blue eyes let him see the world.  His
face had sharp edges to it like a hawk.  Wilson spoke with a booming tone that declared
him to be a leader with an authoritative voice.  Wearing a dark blue uniform with silver
buttons on the jacket, Wilson looked very professional.  He wore large black boots.
Wilson was careful and handy at keeping them very clean and polished until they had a
mirror finish.  A wide gun belt held a .45 semiautomatic in a right side holster.  A dozen
brass bullets filled the belt loops around the back.  A pair of handcuffs was snapped into a
handy location on the left.  His silver police badge was on his chest at the right.  There
were some markings on it at the top denoting that he was the chief of police.  This man
stood and walked like a bull.

The police had heard earlier complaints from the Baxter Mansion guests about some of
their possessions being missing.  Two policemen did visit and take testimonies.  Some of
the rooms and the outdoor yard were searched.  Since none of the bedrooms were looked
over, nothing turned up.  The lost possessions were an open unsolved case.

In the police report the following items were recorded as missing:

> **CITY POLICE MEMORANDUM**
> **Baxter Mansion's Guest's Missing Possessions List:**
>
> Guest:                    Stolen Property:
> Israel Sterling           paper and silver and gold coin money stolen
> Bunny Brompton       deeds contracts stolen
> Florey Filshingham    jewels stolen
> Bertrand E. Hadley    company stock certificates stolen
> Elbert Chessman        rare guns and military medals stolen
> Wyckham Forsythe     bonds stolen

This was a fairly expensive collection of valuables that vanished.  Their owners were confused about loosing them and were wondering just who could have made off with this choice loot.  These six people were both prominent and wealthy individuals.  Each believed that in time the police authorities would find and return each item to its rightful owner.

Time went on.  The six guests had been dealt foul play and never were seen away from Baxter Mansion.  There was some confusion in the nearby town caused by the absence of these six guests.  Usually they made trips into town for recreation, business reasons, or shopping.  They had not been seen in too long a time, nearly three months now.  So suspicions arose as to their whereabouts and the likelihood of heinous cruel foul play.  Different persons contacted the police with their concerns.  Policeman discussed the matter and decided to visit Baxter Mansion and get to the bottom of this thing.

Police Chief Wilson Wallace formed two investigation teams to cover the premises with Lieutenant Bob Bishop and Sergeant Michael Moore as leaders.  One team had five policemen.  The other had six policemen.  They met in two groups.  Their team leaders spoke with them for about ten minutes disbursing directions.  Then they would leave as individuals to move about looking for whatever they might find.  Lieutenant Bishop was a very tall person t 6 foot 6 inches.  Sergeant Moore was rather short at 5 foot 1 inches.  Both men were seasoned veterans with much experience to their credit.  Arriving there they got no answer to ringing the doorbell and knocking on that front door.  The policemen walked about the building peering in through windows for a look at what might be going on inside.  All was quiet.  Peculiarly strange!  There usually were a number of people here moving about inside living a fine life.  Breaking a window glass, one policeman gained entrance.  He opened the front door.  The rest of the investigation squad came inside.  Carefully and cautiously they roamed about the building and the grounds covering in time every nook and cranny.  The dark blue suits of the two police investigation teams moved about the mansion like ants looking for sugar.  Each man did his best exerting his body, using his senses, and putting his wits to the task.  Scouring the place as they did, hope of some new facts that would develop, and some new evidence that would come to hand lured them onward.

Chapter 3.  Robberies and Deaths

The lifeless bodies of the six dead guests were discovered at different places about the mansion.  The murder weapons were found.  Each weapon gave the identity of the murderer being another guest.  This was an odd unexpected discovery that perplexed everyone.  The absence of these people in town was now explained.  Their bedrooms were examined.  Later it came out that each guest had had items stolen from their bedrooms.  Careful searching located these from another guest's bedroom.  Again the investigation showed that another guest took the stolen items.  This created mystery to the crime epoch that had been unfurled.  Here was a mass murder with related robberies by a group of six people with the victims and the suspects being members of the same six of the guests.  This seemed self-contradictory.  This was a difficult puzzle to solve. Photographs, specimens, collection of evidence, and numerous police comments were collected.

All of the stolen personal possessions were found in the different guest's rooms. The police report on this was

**CITY POLICE MEMORANDUM**
**Baxter Mansion Guest's Missing Possessions List and Location Found:**

Owner Guest:  Stolen Property:                     Location Found:
Israel Sterling  paper/silver/gold coin money stolen  Wyckham Forsythe's bedroom
Bunny Brompton  deeds contracts stolen  Elbert Chessman's bedroom
Florey Filshingham  jewels stolen  Bertrand E. Hadley's bedroom
Bertrand E. Hadley  company stock certificates stolen  Florey Filshingham's bedroom
Elbert Chessman  rare guns and military medals stolen  Bunny Brompton's bedroom
Wyckham Forsythe  bonds stolen  Israel Sterling's bedroom

These stolen goods were located in the robber guest's bedroom under a pillow, under the bed, between mattresses, in a chest of drawers, in a wooden storage box in the closet, or in an overcoat pocket hanging in closet.

Then a sharp shock was to occur.  Multiple murders had been committed.  The two police investigation teams found six dead bodies.  These were the six guests of Baxter Mansion. The Police report on these deaths included these persons' names, the room that the corpse was found in, a likely murder weapon, the cause of death, and a clue as to who the murderer was.

**CITY POLICE MEMORANDUM**
**Baxter Mansion Death Report:**


Israel Sterling  garage  tire iron  trauma  Forsythe's gold company token found with a picture of a locomotive and a truck on it
Bunny Brompton  library  sword  lethal body cuts  Chessman's monogrammed engraved name on the sword handle
Florey Filshingham  ballroom  axe  lethal body cuts  Hadley name carved into axe handle
Bertrand E. Hadley  conservatory  arsenic  poisoned  Filshingham's red monogrammed scarf
Elbert Chessman  Chinese room  fireplace poker  trauma  Brompton's business card
Wyckham Forsythe  lounge  rope  strangulation  Sterling's name printed on the rope

A tentative conclusion as to which guest had robbed and murdered another guest was written in another police report.

**CITY POLICE MEMORANDUM**
**Baxter Mansion Crimes Conclusions:**

| Suspect: | | Victim: |
|---|---|---|
| Israel Sterling | robbed and murdered | Wyckham Forsythe |
| Bunny Brompton | robbed and murdered | Elbert Chessman |
| Florey Filshingham | robbed and murdered | Bertrand E. Hadley |
| Bertrand E. Hadley | robbed and murdered | Florey Filshingham |
| Elbert Chessman | robbed and murdered | Bunny Brompton |
| Wyckham Forsythe | robbed and murdered | Israel Sterling |

The police investigation findings indicated that all six guests were robbed and killed by another guest.  The bedroom that the stolen property was found in was that of the same guest that the evidence pointed to that murdered them.  This was a strange conclusion.  An outside suspect was not suggested as the criminal who did all of these crimes, six robberies and six murders.  Bur it was self-contradictory.  How could six dead people rob and kill each other.  The timing sequence for this made it virtually impossible.  The evidence looked phony and not reliable.  The guests were longtime trusting friends who were also related.  There was no motive for them to rob and kill each other.  They were wealthy and stealing was beyond the question for them.  They did not need to steal to live.  They had impressive financial means.

These dead bodies were found in different rooms with evidence that another guest committed each murder.  Clues existed that the very same person who robbed each guest also murdered them.  So now Baxter Mansion had racked up two sets of crimes, robbery and murder.

With the vacation time used up, Robin Baxter and his house service staff returned from their European vacation to learn of the cluster of crimes.  The deaths of his guests were a shock to them all.  Mr. Baxter made this declaration,"It is such a foul catastrophe that has happened here at Baxter Mansion.  Personal property stolen.  The loss of six lives.  These people were the grandest people in my life.  They were also distant relatives.  It does not seem possible.  I hope that the legal authorities will get to the bottom of all this and catch the culprit.  I will now pray for the departed individuals."  In a sad but solemn tone Mr. Baxter spoke the Lord's Prayer.

Chapter 4.  Clues and Investigation

Repeatedly the police went over the mansion, looked at the evidence, read the cause of death statements about the murdered people, held discussions, and tried to understand the crimes as to some likely explanation for what had happened.

The two investigation team leaders gave a summary of their findings speaking to the Police Chief Wilson Wallace.  Lieutenant Bob Bishop said, "We have been over the whole place in a most complete and thorough manner.  Nothing out of the order or conclusive was found.  We found nothing suspicious."  Sergeant Michael Moore then added, "Likewise with our investigation, sir.  We located nothing out of the ordinary."

Who did what to whom?  How?  Why?

Motives were discussed.

What was the motive?  Robbery and murder of six people was a large and serious crime.  There would have to be some good reason for doing all of this.  It was both dangerous and serious crime that when caught up with would deal out a massive punishment in the courts of law.

Motives:
For robbery greed, escape from poverty, pay off debts, hate, envy, revenge, and anger were the usual ones.
For murder jealousy, anger, hatred, lust, sadness, drug or alcohol habit to support, and insanity were the most common ones.

To murder someone, the criminal had to have a strong motive to do this.  Yes, murder was a very serious crime with a severe punishment.

Knives were used for murder crimes more commonly than guns.

Was the evidence genuine or contrived?

Were there other suspects not visible or present that could have been the guilty person, who staged all of this, used deceptive clues to blame innocent guests, and who escaped by leaving the area to move from detection and get safely away?

Mr. Baxter and his servants all had alibis that eliminated them.  The day and time of the crimes was at a time when all of these were away at a vacation with Mr. Baxter.  A steam train then a steam ship took them to Switzerland all summer long for three pleasant months

Mr. Roadway got the black limousine from the garage and drove it to the front door.  Mr. Baxter and his staff put their luggage in the trunk and got inside.  He drove them to the

train station with his cat, Oscar, in his lap.  They bought tickets, checked their baggage
and got aboard a passenger car.  There were steam blasts from locomotive as it started to
leave.  A brass steam whistle shrieked.  There was a shudder as the wheels started to
move.  There were ten passenger cars to pull.  The train started slow.  It crossed over mile
after mile.  In time the train shrunk to a small dot on the distant horizon and vanished.
Mr. Roadway felt lonely and missed the six of them.  The train went to a coastal city to a
steamship terminal.  The travelers bought their tickets, got on the ship, and located their
cabins.  The ship cast off from its dock, smoke came from its smokestacks, and it left the
harbor to sail over an immense ocean.  There was fresh sea air, sunshine, good food, on
deck activities, and a band at night played beautiful music in an auditorium.  This was a
most pleasant voyage.  They landed in France and took a train on to Switzerland.  There
they visited different cities.  There were quaint chalet cottages, scenic mountain views,
exhilarating hikes, green valleys, clean fresh air, aqua blue lakes, delicious food, and
friendly people in a peaceful land.  After about three months' time, the summer was over.
The trip back home was made.  Mr. Robin Baxter and his service staff returned from their
holiday to learn of the sad news about the crimes that had occurred.  The police
eliminated Mr. Baxter and his five house staff as suspects.  The vacationers had all of the
tickets to the trains, ship, and hotels to prove it with names and dates on it.  This was an
ironclad alibi.

They met with the police and listened to all of the sad details.  They were very upset to
learn about the deaths of the guests.

Chapter 5.  Detective George Grubbs

A private detective lived in the nearby city.  George Grubbs was his name.  Aged 40, George smoked cigars.  These were the modest priced drug store type.  He had brown hair, brown eyes and a brown moustache.  He weighed 180 pounds and was a full 6 feet tall.  Usually George wore brown and black suits, wingtip shoes and dark neckties.  There was a .38 pistol in a holster concealed under his left arm.  He kept a leather holder for his silver metal detective badge and license in his pant's pocket.  Mr. Grubbs spoke slowly with a direct solemn a deep gravelly voice that was almost threatening.  As a young man he used to play baseball for a living.  He was a pitcher, center field, and second baseman.  When in the Army he was a policeman.  His office was on the second floor of an office building in the city.  His name was in black paint block letters on the door and three windows.  George Grubbs  Private Investigator.  These items were in that office: a large gray wooden desk and chair, a gray wooden bookcase, a gray metal file cabinet, a fern plant in a clay pot, a framed photograph of him in a baseball uniform pitching in a ball game, a tan stuffed armchair, three boxes of cigars on the file cabinet top, a framed photograph of him in an Army uniform in front of a barracks, a multicolored oval rug, some canned goods and soft drinks in the bookcase, a case of .38 bullets, a cleaning kit for his pistol, and a harmonica.  George drove a seven-year old black four door sedan.

There was much gossip in the air about the foul doings at Baxter Mansion.  Hearing all of this, detective Grubbs' curiosity was aroused.  He came into the case after hearing the rumors.

Police Chief Wilson Wallace met the detective George Grubbs outside the mansion.  He spoke to him at length briefing him about the case details.  They walked about the front of the building to look it over.  Then they walked around together inside to roam about its entirety.

George announced, "Well this is a very classy joint but it is creepy and has a devilish look to it.  Yes, it is old and grand but that added to making it scary."

Police Chief Wallace agreed and added, "Well yes, this would make a great hideout for criminals, a cruel monster's lair, and a place for wicked demons to stay.  All were creatures who did wrongful evil in the world and escaped here for safety and seclusion.  There was no telling who or what has lived here over the years.  It was a shock for me to see this place the first time and walk around inside it.  The whole atmosphere of it makes me uneasy.  It is one spooky and creepy place.  I suppose there have been some nice Halloween parties on these premises.  Successful criminals who had lived here may have hidden their loot in some secret place."

George said loudly, "Well, well, well.  Could you imagine?  Buried treasure!!!"

The Chief observed, "This caper was like a Shakespearean play with a magnificent setting, an impressive cast of characters, and a final scene featuring multiple murders with swords, knives, and poison."

George Grubbs added, "Murder seems to be a common theme with humanity."

There was a silent pause for a while as they strolled about.

George heard the Chief's thoughts and added in conclusion, "The Baxter mansion looked spooky enough that a ghost might want to haunt it."

They spent about three hours examining all that could be seen.  Nothing out of the ordinary or conclusive came up.  A few days later George returned to look it over again by himself.  He read the police reports as well at the autopsy death certificates.  Carefully detective Grubbs reviewed the bedrooms, death scenes and the evidence.  A week later George returned to walk about the building and the grounds another time by himself.

Chapter 6.  Further Investigation

George admitted to himself that he was confused.  The evidence gave to solution to what had happened.  It conflicted itself.  The guests were alone with each other.  The goods stolen from the people who lived here were all left with some evidence that another guest stole them.  Each murder likewise had concrete clues that another guest did the killings.  But how could dead people have stolen and murdered each other?  This was nonsense.  Obviously there was false evidence to confuse the law and conceal the identity of the actual guilty culprit.  A magnificent deception!

Detective George Grubbs just could not add all of this up and arrive at a certain bottom line total for what had happened.  Thinking about it was frustrating and repeatedly doing so gave him a headache.  It was like a Chinese finger puzzle.  The harder you pulled on it the tighter it got.  So he continued to look over official papers, talk to the police, and move around looking over all that was here at the mansion.

Detective Grubbs walked over and looked at the lands about the mansion and that out a ways past the yard.  He inspected the lawn, flowerbeds, shrubs, trees, drain culverts, some large rocks that were present, the three fountains, the benches, and the driveway.  Closer to the building, he walked just beside it, and took a close look at the outside walls, the foundation, windows, doors, the front and rear porches, the roof, chimney, copula, and gutters.  All of this being done, he next continued inside.  In each room he examined the walls, ceiling, floor, light fixtures, doors which included their sides, hinges, knobs, locks, and jambs, windows which involved their glass panes, mullions, locks, and curtains, wall next to each window, closets, shelves, and all of the furniture.  In the kitchen he studied the appliances, shelved, cabinets, sinks, and the stored food items.  In the laundry Mr. Grubbs scoured its appliances, piled up soiled clothing and bedding waiting to be washed, and the cleaning substances in pasteboard boxes and bottles.  In the bathrooms he looked over the bathtubs, sinks, toilets, shelves, and the medicine cabinets with mirrors.  In the basement he surveyed the heating equipment, plumbing pipes, drains, flues, and the electrical apparatus.  In the attic he looked at the floor, roof, and stored items.  Finally he went over the stairways, fireplaces, the firewood, and the coal piles. George liked to scratch things with his three bladed pocketknife and tap different objects with it to see how they sounded, solid or hollow.  There was nothing odd, peculiar, or suspicious in the entire house.

He smiled when a new idea suddenly came to him.  Maybe there was a secret room, passageway, in the house where the suspect stayed, went in and out of, made his attack from, and escaped after committing the crimes.  If it led from the building, it would allow him to escape, assume a disguise or false name, and go far away to freedom undetected.  Looking for this, he found nothing.  His new idea was discarded.

George Grubbs thought that there were some likely places that things in the house might have been used as weapons. The kitchen had knives. The Chinese room had centuries old weapons. There were swords, knives, spears, bows and arrows, and this spiked ball attached to a chain to a wooden handle. The garage tool room had many things like sledgehammers, axes, knives, and hatchets that were possible death weapons. He visited these rooms, looked these over, and found nothing likely to have been used in the six murders.

Policemen were dependable professionals. They were respected at their work. In this situation they made one mistake. They did not check the six stolen goods and the murder weapons for fingerprints. It the six guests did commit the robberies and murders, it would be expected that their fingerprints would be on them. The murder weapons were these: tire iron, sword, axe, bottle of arsenic, fireplace poker, and a rope. George Grubbs fingerprinted the corpses, the stolen goods, and the weapons. The rope was the exception. Its coarse texture made checking it for prints impossible. The guest fingerprints were not on the stolen goods or the murder weapons. Detective Grubbs decided that guests did not commit the robberies and that the murder weapons were not used to kill the people. They were fakes planted to lead the law astray. Who did this and why was a mystery.

George Grubbs met again with Police Chief Wallace to discuss the case.

George said, "I have made other examinations of the premises. I found nothing that added anything. It all looked very normal. I fingerprinted the bodies, the stolen items, and the murder weapons. The stolen property and the weapons had no prints on them. This puts doubt that the robberies were made by the guests and that the murder weapons were not used by the guests to kill the other guests. Some phony goings on are at foot. This entire case is too cloudy to see through. Nothing makes any sense."

Police Chief Wallace spoke, "Yes, our searches deed little else too. Fingerprints! That was one thing we forgot about. Good for you to think of it. You say the prints give no positive evidence? That is odd. What we see and what really is conflicts. This is a puzzling case that has the lot of us stumped."

After spending time looking the case, George concluded that nothing out of order was found. No new clues that pointed to the crimes were found. His mind went reeling. What else could he now do? Re-examine it all? Widen the search to more distant places?

To himself quietly George Grubbs thought, "There did seem to me to be a mystery to Baxter Mansion. What had caused the robberies and deaths? No certain answer had been located."

Chapter 7. A Frightening Discovery

George walked from the mansion's porch out over the rear long open lawn to its left side along a dirt pathway where the grass was worn away.  He went on a long arc that sloped downwards.  Crossing along he came to level area where a Chinese holly shrub made a square of about forty feet.  What this was could be anybody's guess.  It was a quiet place for a picnic.  Eating here in the fresh air would be pleasant.  Somehow the air seemed to suddenly chill.  The air seemed denser too.  This made George become frightened as if something was watching him.  Why he felt this way, he did not know.  George looked the grounds over.  From here on there was some more lawn and then the thick forest.  There was nothing to what was here.  So he returned to the mansion.

In the kitchen he found coffee and fresh bread buns.  He sat down at a table.  Helping himself he became refreshed.  Lighting a cigar, he puffed on it for a time to enjoy the rich strong taste of the tobacco.  His mind went blank.  He subconsciously thought over the case.  What should he do next?  Where should he go in search of clue leads and further evidence?  His mind wound on and on.  Walking along a hallway George made his way into the conservatory.  This was a most pleasant room with numerous fresh green plants that perfumed the air.  The glassed in ceiling let in the moonlight.  The door out led to a terrace paved with a brick floor.  Crossing this, George passed over a lawn to a spa.  It was a heated indoor pool that experts claim to be most healthy.  This had stone half walls and that were glassed at the top.  The roof was also glass.  Doors on each end could be opened.  The roof could be cranked back.  The spa could be in pleasant weather opened to the outside air.  Fresh air would add to the enjoyment of the spa.  Passing this was a clay tennis court with a ten-foot high green metal screen fence.  Two dark green wooden benches were just outside the fence on the side nearest to the spa.  There was nothing past this but open lawn.  George looked all of this over for some available clue.  None was found.

He returned to the mansion.  A walk around the side of the building just past the shrub beds might be a good idea.  George walked past the conservatory side, along the front, to turn to the far side.  Here the boxwood shrub bed continued.  Three oak trees grew here too.  A George walked forward a knocking sound was heard.  One of the oak tree limbs was hitting the outside wall of the building making the noise.  At first this frightened George.  As he walked up to it, he saw what it was, smiled, and relaxed.  Turning at the corner he came to the back yard where squared off shrubs continued.  There was a fountain and some sculpture here.  A carefully planted and cared for flowerbed gave much color there.  Then from a distance something strange came into view.  A cloudy form was hovering a few feet above the hedge.  It was tornado shaped and spinning about.  The cloud mostly was silent.  A strange swishing sound was heard as it hovered.  Swirling flashing lights poured from it colored white, silver, pale yellow, metallic blue, and gold.  Then breaking the quiet, it said this, "Areeee Areeee Aroooo."  It was a funnel shaped being with a head, torso, and narrowed into a long tail.  There was a face with a large nose, big cheeks, and a thick chin.  It had hair.  The chest was covered in a dark suit jacket with a collared shirt and a necktie.  It was all hues of dark gray and difficult to see any detail.  The creature faced George.  George stopped when he saw it.  For a time they looked each other over.  Mr. Grubbs was frightened for his safety and well being.  The creature's tail stub at the bottom twitched.  Then quickly it came towards George, rose above his head, and flew up the wall to disappear over the roof.  This attacking and leaving flight of the funnel creature made George terrified.  The thing came at him very fast.  This had been a short glimpse.  But that had been enough.  Now Mr. Grubbs had a new observation at the mansion to think about.  Was this part of his case?  It was like something that he never had seen before.

Chapter 8.  Lightning

A few nights later George decided to look around some more.  He had spent time
thinking over what he saw earlier, the funnel monster.  The direction that it flew to may
be a lead.  There was a pathway in that direction, as he could remember leading from the
lawn into the woods.  It was a dark night that being rather cool had an excess of moisture
in the air.  Many stars dotted the sky with tiny glowing light flashes.  A nearly full moon
put much eerie light on everything.  Detective George Grubbs walked out of the mansion
from the front doorway to pass over the green yard along a gravel walkway.  After many
steps were made, he entered the woods.  The moonlight in these trees was a spectacular
sight.  The woods lasted about three fourths of a mile.  It was an open field that ranged
far away into the distance.  Walking on he passed much land.  There in front appeared a
black iron fence.  It went around about fifty tombstones.  This was an old mostly
abandoned cemetery.

A few years ago a rainstorm came up in the winter when snow covered the ground almost
a foot deep.  Thunder and lightning went on for over an hour.  One large lightning bolt
came down to the earth to strike the metal graveyard fence.  It arced over and hit a nearby
tombstone at the top where a metal cross was mounted.  This knocked a pie slice chip
from one side of the headstone.  Some of the material was heated and burnt.  Soot and
small cracks covered stained this side where the snow was vaporized and the headstone
was heated very hot.  The iron fence conducted electricity through the ground for some
sizeable distance.  Minerals were in the earth.  These were silica, quartz, mica, salt,
sodium, magnesium, manganese, and sulfur.  There was marsh gas due to clay materials
present.  This matter was heated and fused together into a glassy mass.  The grass and the
soil were burnt.  A nearby tree and several shrubs were scorched and killed.  The
electricity from the lightning passed into the soil and went about the nearest casket.  The
dead body inside received huge blast of electrical power.  This shock energized the spirit
of that dead human.  Electricity built up inside the metal casket and was stored there for
months.  This was a powerful mass of static electricity.  This over time created a static
electrical spirit made from the ghost of that dead person.

Detective Grubbs looked the cemetery over extremely carefully.  He examined all the
markers, the earth, and the iron fence.  He noticed where lightning had struck the fence,
the fused glassy minerals in the ground, dead shrubs and tree, and the damaged
tombstone.  Likely a large lightning bolt had hit this location.  How it hit the fence, the
soil, and the tombstone was puzzling to him.  Obviously it bounced from the fence to the
grave marker.  Could this be where the funnel creature came from?  There was a name
and dates on the damaged tombstone.  Writing this down, George wanted to learn about
who this was buried here and all that he could about him.  Could lightning have created
this ghost by charging the buried body?  This idea kept coming back to him.  Did he
guess correctly that this was the grave of the ghost he saw the other night?  The name on
the marker was Jack Larson.  Researching this he discovered that the man was an Army
major who fought in the war.  Wounds put him in a hospital for nearly a year.  A blow to
his head made him crazy.  His doctors did not find this out.  He healed and was released

from the hospital to be put back into the battle fighting. His fellow soldiers noticed that he did odd things and was less than his usual self. Major Jack Larson ordered twenty of them to attack an enemy position that as very dangerous. All twenty-one soldiers died. He was later buried here. Before the war started, he had owned the Baxter mansion. George found out that the ghost who belonged to a crazy man might itself, be crazy. George also reasoned that jealous of those living, and being in his former house he resented them. So it stole from them and later murdered them. The static electricity ghost theory might explain the flashing metallic quicksilver colors that the funnel ghost had. It looked like sparkling sparking smoke. The light of the colors went on an off. Static charges did this. Maybe the lightning created a ghost from the dead man's body from static electricity. Lightning had released his ghost as a static electricity vortex funnel. This ghost was made of static electricity which was charges that do not move. Negative ions massed together from a magnetic field. He concluded that possibly static electricity was the gears, springs, and wires that made the funnel ghost work. George later read that ghosts make magnetic field changes. This caused sparking. The smell of ozone was present. Static electricity!! Well, well, well. This may be something at last.

Detective Grubbs returned several times to this cemetery to look it all over much more closely. He looked for anything suspicious.

At the mansion's library George found books on ghosts. He read about them. There were five kinds of ghosts:

Type 1. Ghosts from a dead person. These are the floating sheet type of ghost. They may become visible and make sounds, move things, speak, touch you, release odors like perfumes, tobacco, smoke, or foul putrid fumes to tell you they were present. These ghosts may look like and keep the personality of the former living person that they had when they were alive. They may be able to feel emotions. Dead people ghosts might make visits to people for different reasons like to comfort them or to say something important.

Type 2. Ectoplasm ghosts were moving, whirling, fog, smoky, mist, haze that were cloud like. Usually they stayed near to the ground. These can stay still or may move very fast. Mostly ectoplasms were gray, white, or black in color. Ectoplasmic forms may appear before a real ghost came into view. They may be seen in old houses, graveyards, and battlefields.

Type 3. Poltergeists were the most popular and common type of ghost but were really rare. The word meant a noisy ghost as they made sounds. They could move things like slamming doors and shutters, chalk chains and anchors, lift and drop glass to break it, and knock things over. Poltergeists could act on real things to create a disturbance, turn on and off lights, or start fires. They caused events that started slowly and quietly, gradually increased in speed and intensity, and then vanished suddenly. These events were usually harmless but may become destructive or even deadly dangerous. Poltergeists may be caused unknowingly by a living person as subconscious wishes.

Type 4. Orbs were a clear ball of light that stayed still above the ground. They were thought by some to be the spirit of a dead person or an animal that was traveling about. Their rounded shape made moving easy for them so they could move fast. Orbs may be the first state of a ghost that later changed form to be seen easier by humans. Since they were light, these were photographed easily commonly appearing as white or blue light.

Type 5. A funnel ghost was a vortex that was narrow at the bottom, and wide at the top. They swirled from rotation, tornado shaped. They were ghosts returning to visit people, buildings, or a place as they were long past residents there that died or left. On photographs they resembled spiraling waves of light.

After reading this, Detective Grubbs thought to himself, "The form I saw was the funnel ghost type. Yes, this is certain. The tail narrowed into a funnel about four feet long like the part of a tornado that was near to the ground."

This ghost suspect idea was wacky but maybe still possible. The ghost did the robberies and murders. It made the false evidence to escape being detected and blamed. So George Grubbs had eliminated the false clues. They were too contradictory to be real and true. So he changed his methods of examination to look for other clues. These were focused on the ghost.

In his city office, George Grubbs drank hot black coffee and munched on several doughnuts on a dish. The sugary frosting was delicious. Several of them were crème and cherry jelly-filled. His belly was filled with an enjoyable delight. Cleaning his lips and fingers with a napkin, he sat back in his chair to look out a window at the day. Reaching into a pocket, he pulled out a cigar. Lighting his, he drew in several puffs, blew smoke out into the room, and relaxed further. His thoughts kept rebounding off of the unsolved Baxter Mansion crimes.

The police reports provided possibly conflicting evidence to robberies and the murders. Yes, it was evidence yielded directly from the crime scenes. It was genuine first hand material. It was factual police work documentation to the crimes. George Grubbs rejected all of it as some fantastic scheme placed to throw the police off the track. It was planted to divert their attention from the truth and another criminal agent so far unseen and undetected by the long arm of the law. All of that was a delightful, devious deception. George pondered about the ghost sighting. He figured it as an idea to work on. How could you get evidence on a ghost? How could you catch it? Could it be destroyed? If so what then would be the consequences? Although it was not likely easily provable as the real killer suspect, he must try different methods and create different strategies to solve the case. So he would look the mansion over for better clues that may be related to the ghost ore some other possibility. How could he find the ghost? Detective Grubbs must decide what was real evidence and what obviously was false evidence. The clues that the murdered people robbed and killed each other was too conflicting. How could this have happened? It could not have! Baxter mansion was very old, creepy, and spooky. Yes, a ghost would like to visit and stay there. Maybe a ghost did do the robberies and killings. How could he find and see it? He spent more time in Baxter Mansion secretly; just hoping to see and catch the ghost before it did more harm.

Chapter 9.  Capture

George Grubbs was shocked but pleased in his discovery of the funnel ghost.  He did not
tell anyone even the police as they may mess up the case for him.  It was his secret.  It
was better this way as telling the truth may scare people.  He figured it did the crimes.
George made plans to photograph, catch, and destroy it.

He soon found out that the ghost was invisible on film.  It was immune to photography.
Maybe he could dye it and then make a photograph.  He never figured out how to dye it.
He did spray ink about the lawn hoping to stain the funnel creature but it never appeared.
So he gave this up.  He planned to shoot, poison, gas, dynamite, burn, club, or scare it
with loud noises.  He toyed with a magnifying glass, water splashed on it to short circuit
static charges, trap it between mirrors, shock it with high voltage electricity, attack it with
dogs, and trap it in big steel tank.  These ideas he came up with but never did anything
with them.  It was an elusive ghost that moved fast and was not dependable to get to
appear when and where he wanted.

Detective George Grubbs concluded that it would not be possible to arrest a ghost, try it
in court, and then to sentence it.  So it would be better to get a foolproof method to trap
and destroy it.  This would be legal, merciful, and just.  It would have to also be safe and
freed from harming him and others.  Then no more horrors could happen.  For several
weeks he came up with ideas that he could not use, that would not work.  And he
discarded them.  At last he had a good one.  Detective Grubbs bought a large extremely
fine copper mesh screen.  It was nearly invisible.  He hung it up from slender wires
outside of Baxter Mansion in the back lawn near where he first sighted the ghost.  From
the screen he ran away seven wires that were grounded to steel rods driven deep into the
earth.  He saturated the soil around the rods with a mineral alt solution to enhance
conduction.

One night near midnight he was staked out hidden in the shrubbery with a green sheet
about him as camouflage.  The funnel ghost of Jack Larsen did appear.  It came over the
roof and descended down the wall to hover above the hedge.  It stayed still about half an
hour.  Then finally it moved forward and struck the invisible copper screen.  There was
flashing blue lights and a loud electrical popping sound.  A five-foot hole was burned in
the screen from the heat.  The static charges on the ghost were destroyed.  They were
strong but were successfully drained away.  The ghost was dead and gone.  Static
electricity powered it and made it alive.  It dematerialized never to reappear again.
George Grubbs had met with success.  He was elated and proud of what he had
accomplished.  He wrote a length and detailed report.  A copy of it he gave to police
Chief Wilson Wallace.  Over doughnuts and hot coffee the two of them discussed the
case in the chief's office.  The police chief was befuddled and amazed to learn now that
the criminal had been a crazy ghost.  He was proud of the efforts by detective George
Grubbs.

Chapter 10.  Recovery

Jack Larson's funnel ghost creature was now gone.  It roamed no more.  Baxter mansion was free of this evil.  No further harm would be done.  The stolen items reappeared it the rooms of the guests from where they were found missing.  The murder weapons stored at the police station likewise vanished.  Each of the dead people reappeared alive and unharmed.  They came back to life at night sleeping in heir beds.  This was the kindest way for them to be returned as living creatures.  Sleeping people see, hear, and feel nothing.  So only at awakening the next day do they return to the life of the living.  None of them ever knew they were murdered and dead.  It was as if they were never killed.  They had to be told of the mysterious happenings that occurred.  They were completely unaware of what had happened.  Or seemed to have happened.  All of these guests were healthy and unharmed.  All of this was proof that the crazy ghost of Jack Larson was the criminal that stole and killed.  The case finally was solved.

The spell cast by Jack Larson's ghost was broken.  This was a delusion the ghost created to frighten and confuse the living people.  It was a crazy spook's method of getting revenge for his jealousy of their being alive and living in what once was his home.  Mr. Baxter went to Jack Larson's gravesite with his house staff and guests.  They held prayer sessions there.  This was done to remove the evil that might be present so no more threatening crimes would occur.  In the years to come peace reigned.  No more did Jack Larson's spirit return.  No more fictitious crimes happened.  The threat was destroyed.

The End